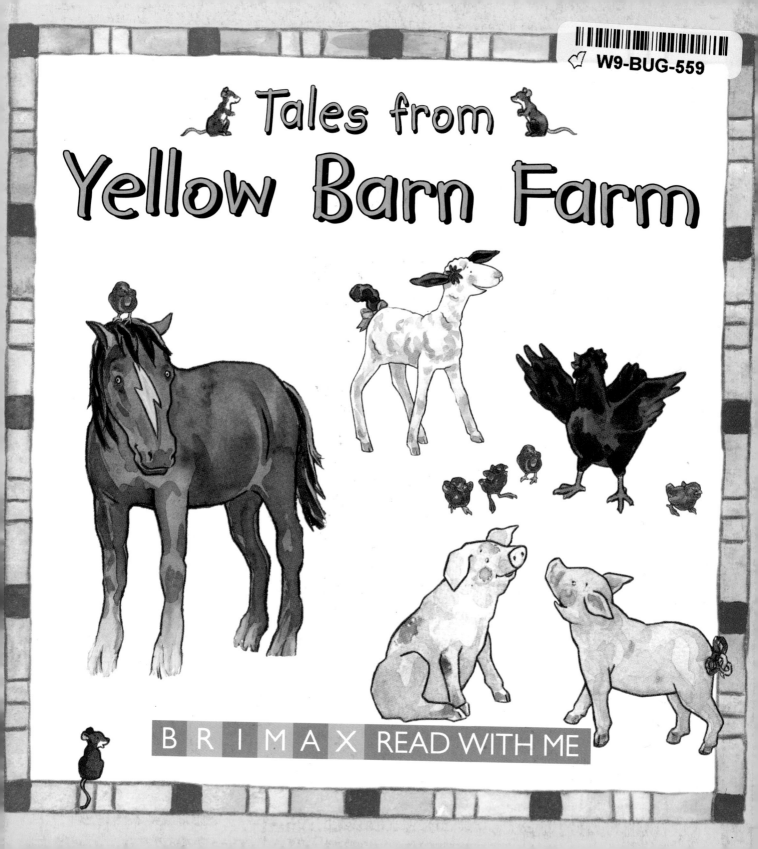

Tales from Yellow Barn Farm

BRIMAX READ WITH ME

Words by Gill Davies
Pictures by Tina Freeman
First published in Great Britain in 2001 by Brimax
This edition published in 2002 by Brimax
an imprint of Octopus Publishing Group Ltd
2-4 Heron Quays, London, E14 4JP
© Octopus Publishing Group Ltd

ISBN 1 85854 288 X

Printed in China

Contents

Lucy Lamb

Lucy Lamb

It is Spring on Yellow Barn Farm.

"Moo!" says Mrs Cow. "I hear that the bluebells in Ferny Wood are wonderful this year."

"Baa!" says Lucy Lamb.
"I should like to hear them."

So Lucy trots along the lane until she comes to Ferny Wood.

Then Lucy stands. She looks around and listens.

Lucy can see lots of beautiful blue flowers swaying gently in the breeze.

But she cannot hear any bells!

Just then, Foxy Cub peeps through the trees.

"Where do the bluebells ring?" asks Lucy.

"I don't know," says Foxy, "but I should like to hear them."

So Lucy trots further into the wood and Foxy Cub scampers after her.

Just then, Squirrel peeps through the leaves.

"Do you know where the bluebells ring?" asks Lucy.

"No," says Squirrel, "but it would be fun to find out."

So Lucy trots further into the wood, and Foxy Cub and Squirrel scamper after.

Just then, Sukie Rabbit peeps
through the bracken.

"Do the bluebells ring here?"
asks Lucy.

"I have no idea," says Sukie,
"but I should like to know."

So Lucy trots further into the wood,
and Foxy, Squirrel and Sukie
scamper after her.

Just then, Oliver Otter scrambles up the river bank. He wants to know what all the trotting and scampering is about!

"Can you tell us where the bluebells ring?" asks Lucy.

Oliver begins to smile. His smile gets wider and wider, and then he begins to laugh.

"Bluebells don't ring," laughs Oliver, rolling on the grass and holding his tummy.

"They are flowers. They are all around you. Look!"

The animals look at the bell shapes of the beautiful blue flowers.

Then they look back at Oliver rolling on the grass.

Very soon, Lucy, Foxy, Squirrel and Sukie are rolling on the grass and laughing, too!

When all the animals stop laughing, they all agree that Mrs Cow is right about the bluebells…

They are really wonderful this year!

**Here are some words
in the story.
Can you read them?**

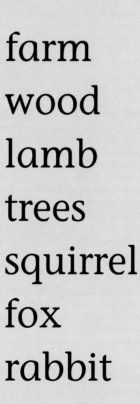

farm	otter
wood	bluebells
lamb	Spring
trees	trots
squirrel	ring
fox	river
rabbit	cow

How much of the story can you remember?

Who tells Lucy Lamb that the bluebells in Ferny Wood are wonderful this year?

Lucy can't hear the bells in Ferny Wood, but what can she see lots of?

Which three animals help Lucy to find the bluebells?

What are their names?

Who tells Lucy and her friends that bluebells are flowers?

Can you spot five differences
in these pictures?

Two Naughty Piglets

Two Naughty Piglets

Polly and Percy Piglets live
on Yellow Barn Farm.

They don't mean to be naughty–
but somehow, they always are!

Today they are very excited
because Farmer Jones has
a new red tractor.

"Shall we see if Farmer Jones will give us a ride in his tractor?" snorts Percy.

The two little piglets trot into the farmyard.

There is the red tractor – all new and shiny.

But Farmer Jones is nowhere to be seen!

The two naughty piglets know that they should wait for Farmer Jones, but Percy is too excited.

"Let's sit inside," he says to Polly, and he jumps up into the tractor.

"This is great," Percy shouts.

Polly is too short to climb up.

"Please help me," she squeaks, standing on tiptoe.

Percy leans down and pulls Polly up into the tractor, but he slips!

The naughty piglets tumble down inside the tractor.

Somehow, they undo the brake!

The tractor begins to move.
It rolls across the farmyard.

"Help!" squeaks Polly.

"Help!" squeals Percy.

"Help!" squawk the hens, flapping
all over the farmyard.

Feathers fly everywhere as turkeys
and cockerels flap out of the way!

The tractor rolls into the barn
and crashes into the hay.

The barn is in a terrible
mess when the tractor stops.

Farmer Jones rushes into the barn and sees all the mess.

"You naughty little piglets!" shouts Farmer Jones. "No mud baths for a whole week."

"We're very, very sorry!" say Polly and Percy, shaking. They are very scared.

The naughty piglets scamper away as fast as their legs can carry them.

Polly and Percy go to their sty and lie down in the hay.

"From now on, we will always try to be good little piglets," they grunt.

Here are some words
in the story.
Can you read them?

farm	hens
piglet	turkey
farmer	cockerels
red tractor	barn
jump	hay
feathers	sty

How much of the story can you remember?

What is new at Yellow Barn Farm?

Who jumps into the tractor first?

What does the tractor do?

Where does the tractor stop?

What does Farmer Jones say to the piglets?

What do the piglets promise to do?

Can you match the pictures to make four pairs?

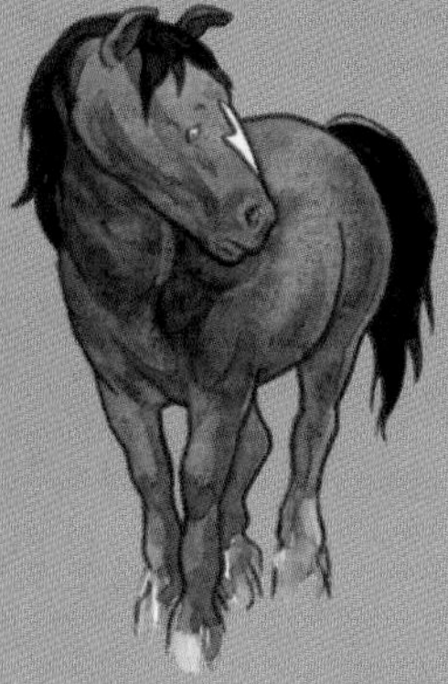

A Friend
for Flash

A Friend for Flash

Flash feels lonely. He feels lonely because he is the only horse on Yellow Barn Farm.

"It is alright for those cows," he sighs. "There are lots of other cows in the field. They can all moo and play together all day long."

Flash wanders over to the next field.

"It is alright for those sheep," sighs
Flash. "There are lots of other sheep
in the field. They can baa and
play together all day long.
But I am the only horse."

Flash wanders over to the farmyard.

"It is alright for those geese," sighs
Flash. "There are lots of other geese
in the farmyard. They can honk
and play games all day long.
But I am a lonely, only horse."

Flash wanders back to his field. He thinks of all the other lucky animals on Yellow Barn Farm.

"There are lots of pigs to grunt together, lots of hens to cluck together, and lots of ducks to quack together. But there is only one of me!"

Tears start to fall from Flash's eyes.

Ben, the wise, kind scarecrow, sees Flash crying and peeps over the hedge.

"You're not the only one who is a lonely one," says Ben.
"I am the only scarecrow."

"True," says Flash, shaking his tears away.

"Cheer up," says Ben. "No-one needs to be lonely on Yellow Barn Farm."

"Really?" asks Flash.

"Of course!" says Ben. "You can be friends with all of the animals. You can play with the cows and the sheep, the geese and the pigs, the hens and the ducks, and all the other animals on the farm."

"And best of all," says Ben,
"you can play with me! I have
a broomstick leg and I can only
hop about slowly, so you can give
me rides."

Flash looks at Ben's one, wooden
leg, and then looks at his own four,
fast legs.

Flash knows just how lucky he is.

"Would you like a ride now?"
asks Flash.

"Ooh, yes please," says Ben, and
on he hops.

Now the two of them are great
friends. Flash gives Ben rides every
day as they visit all their new
friends on Yellow Barn Farm.

Flash is never lonely now.

Here are some words
in the story.
Can you read them?

horse	geese
farm	pigs
cows	hens
field	ducks
sheep	tears
farmyard	scarecrow

How much of the story can you remember?

What sort of animal is Flash?

Why is Flash lonely?

What can the cows do all day long?

What can the sheep do all day long?

What can the geese do all day long?

Who peeps over the hedge to talk to Flash?

Who is Ben great friends with at the end of the story?

Help Flash to find a route
so that he can give Ben a ride.

Happy Hen

Happy Hen

It is morning on Yellow Barn Farm.

The cockerel crows, the cows moo, the pigs oink, and the lambs baa. It is very noisy!

"Sshhhh!" says Happy Hen. "My eggs are sleeping." Then she sits down and sings a song to her eggs.

That night, Happy Hen whispers to her eggs.

"Yellow Barn Farm is a wonderful place. Soon you will hatch. Then you will be able to see for yourselves."

And then Happy Hen sings a lullaby to her sleepy eggs before she falls asleep, too.

The next morning it is time for the eggs to hatch.

Peck! Peck! Peck! Ten little beaks break open the shells.

Squeak! Squeak! Squeak! Ten little chicks tumble out.

"Welcome to Yellow Barn Farm," moos Mrs Cow, who has come to see the chicks.

Soon the little chicks are scampering and flapping all over the farmyard.

"Squeak! Squeak! Squeak!" they all chirp happily.

"Oink! Oink! Oink!" says a happy piglet to the chicks.

The chicks follow their mother everywhere, and copy everything she does.

Happy Hen laughs... so do ten little chicks.

Happy Hen dances... so do ten little chicks – but three fall over!

And when Happy Hen sings, ten little chicks sing, too.

And now, every morning, all the
farm animals sing songs.

The cockerel crows, Mrs Cow
moos, the little piglets oink, and
Lucy Lamb baas.

And Happy Hen clucks and chirps
with her ten little chicks.

And every night, all the animals sing lullabies.

The mice squeak, the owls hoot, and the cats miaow.

And Happy Hen tweets and twitters with her ten little chicks.

Yellow Barn Farm is even noisier than ever, but now it is full of songs and lullabies.

Farmer Jones looks around at his farm and smiles to himself.

What a happy Yellow Barn Farm this is!

Here are some words in the story. Can you read them?

farm	eggs
cockerel	chicks
cows	farmyard
pigs	mice
piglets	owls
lambs	cats
hen	farmer

How much of the story can you remember?

What does the cockerel do in the morning on Yellow Barn Farm?

What are the eggs doing at the beginning of the story?

What does Happy Hen sing to her eggs before she falls asleep?

What tumbles out of the eggs?

Is Yellow Barn Farm noisy?

Who looks around the farm and smiles?

Read with me in words and pictures

Happy Hen lives in a  .

Every morning the crows,

the moo,

the oink

and the baa!

Happy Hen has ten  .

Soon the eggs hatch into  .

The  flap all

over the .

At night the is very noisy.

The squeak, the

hoot and the miaow!

Notes for parents

Tales From Yellow Barn Farm is a delightful collection of animal adventures, designed to expand your child's vocabulary and improve reading and recognition skills. With your help, reading can also be a source of great enjoyment. These handy guidelines will help you and your child to get maximum fun and educational benefit from this collection.

- **Key words** are listed at the end of each story for your child to repeat and remember. Why not go back to the story and ask your child to find the key word and corresponding illustration, and see what they have learnt? Then see if they are able to make up new sentences of their own, using the key words.

- A **questions section** also allows you to see how much of the story your child has understood and can recall easily. You may want to supplement this with questions of your own where appropriate.